When We Went WILD

Isabella Tree
& Allira Tee

iVY KiDS

Nancy and Jake were farmers.
They plowed their fields and planted crops.
They milked their cows and fed their pigs.
They did what all good farmers do.

They sprayed chemicals on the crops to help them grow,

Sprayed more chemicals to kill the insects that might eat the crops,

and even more chemicals to kill the weeds and thistles that grew in between.

They bought big, expensive machines to help them spray and harvest the crops and milk the cows. The machines looked like something from a space station!

But even though they tried to do everything right, the pigs
looked sad. The cows looked sad. Even the trees looked sad.
No flowers grew, no bees buzzed, and when it rained
all the animals had to stay inside, as the fields
turned to sticky, stuggy, stodgy mud.

When the bills for all the chemicals and the big,
expensive machines came in, Jake and Nancy looked sad too.
"I don't know how we're going to pay these," Jake said.

One day, among the bills, a glossy brochure arrived.
It was for a wild animal safari in Africa. The animals and
the tourists looked like they were having a lovely time.
But an expensive holiday was beyond Jake
and Nancy's wildest dreams.

But then, Nancy had an idea.
"If we can't go to the wilderness,
let's bring it here! Let's go wild!"

So, they sold the big, shiny
machines, and they sold
the metal drums full
of chemicals,

and with the money, they paid their bills.

Then, they waited.

It didn't take long for things to change.

With the chemicals gone, wildflowers sprang up,
and bees, butterflies, and beetles hummed
and buzzed in the air.

Without the constant plowing,
the land didn't turn to mud. Messy tangles
of brambles and wild roses grew, and birds made
their nests among the thorns. Even nightingales that had
flown all the way from Africa returned to sing their burbling song!

The cows and the pigs thought it was the best thing ever. The cows loved nibbling the tasty leaves from the bushes. The pigs plunged into ponds and got fat, gorging on worms and acorns. They didn't miss their shed one bit. Nancy and Jake were so happy, they thought everyone would be happy too.

But their neighbors were not pleased at all.
"Look at the mess they've made. It's
nothing but brambles and weeds!"

"They've ruined our view."

"It's so noisy!
The birds keep me
awake at night."

They wrote angry letters to the local newspaper.

The FARM LIFE Weekly

Wildflowers Ruining Landscape

Too much nature on this country farm

Nancy and Jake were really worried.

They might be forced to use chemicals again. The wildflowers,
the bees, the butterflies, and the birds would all disappear, and the
cows and pigs would go back into their sheds and be sad.
They wondered what to do.

Then, a terrible storm
blew in. It began
to rain—

and rain—

and rain.
All around, rivers were
bursting their banks.

People's homes were flooded, and cars
and motorbikes bobbed downstream.

BREAKING NEWS RAIN BRINGS FLASH FLOODING ACROSS THE COUNTRY

In a panic, the neighbors built walls of
sandbags around their homes, as they
prepared for the floods to reach them.

But the flood never came. The rain stopped, and the farm and the village looked like nothing had ever happened. All the new trees and flowers on the farm had drunk up the rain.

The unplowed soil had soaked in the water like a sponge and protected the houses around the farm. The neighbors scratched their heads. "Perhaps going wild is a good thing after all," they thought.

They began to enjoy the birdsong and the insects buzzing, and they laughed at the pigs splashing about in the ponds.

They stopped using chemicals in their gardens to kill the insects and weeds, and stopped mowing their lawns all the time.

They let the grass grow and stopped trimming
the hedges back to the bone. They looked around
at the trees and hedges, bursting into life.

"What were we thinking?" they said.

"Let's all go wild!"

A note on "rewilding"

Dear Reader,

I hope you've enjoyed this story. You might be wondering, are Jake and Nancy real? Is this a true story? Jake and Nancy are made-up characters, but their story is based on a number of real examples, including our own.

Back in 2000, my husband Charlie and I rewilded our farm called Knepp in West Sussex, UK. We weren't making money because our soil is really bad for farming. So, we stopped plowing the fields and milking cows in farm buildings, and instead allowed cows, ponies, pigs, and deer to roam free on our land. Astonishing things happened. Wildlife returned, just like in the story, and our soil was full of tiny creatures again.

The farm I imagined for this story is probably a hill farm. Wild land can hold on to huge amounts of water when it rains, like a sponge, even on steep slopes. But on farms where the soil has been plowed again and again, and all the little creatures that live in it have been killed by chemicals, water can't sink in. It just runs over the soil straight into rivers which then break their banks. So, letting land go wild really can help protect houses and people from flooding.

More and more farmers have been inspired to rewild their land, which means letting it go to a more "natural" state, and sometimes reintroducing big or extinct animals.

People often ask me, how can we grow enough food if lots of farms go wild? The truth is, we already produce more than enough food globally for everyone, but we waste at least 30% of it, scraping food off our plates into the trash. We won't buy vegetables that don't look completely perfect, and we feed expensive grain to cows even though they'd rather eat grass. If we stop wasting food, we can give a lot of land back to nature.

But even on good farmland, we need to take better care of the soil or soon it won't be able to grow anything. If we farm with nature, allowing the soil to recover, letting insects pollinate our crops and control pests instead of using chemicals, we'll be able to grow enough food for ourselves without destroying the environment, and the food will be more nutritious, too. This is called regenerative farming.

We can do both—farm in a better way, and rewild all the areas in between, from hillsides to city parks and roadside shoulders, from orchards and churchyards to backyards and window boxes—we can all do our bit for a wilder, happier world.

Isabella Tree

At Ivy Kids, we know that our readers will inherit the world we create, and we owe it to them to be constantly improving the sustainability of our publishing process.

The paper this book is printed on is certified by the Forest Stewardship Council as made from 100% post-consumer waste, meaning no new trees have been felled to make it, and less water is used compared to virgin paper production. This book can be recycled.

It has been printed in the USA, meaning emissions from shipping have been reduced as far as possible.

By buying a copy of this book, you have made a choice to support a more eco-friendly way of publishing, thank you.

Text © 2021 Isabella Tree. Illustrations © 2021 Allira Tee.
Beautiful Demoiselle and Hawk Moth images by Neil Hulme.
Other photos by Charlie Burrell.

First published in 2021 by Ivy Kids, an imprint of The Quarto Group.
100 Cummings Center, Suite 265D, Beverly, MA 01915, USA.
T +1 978-282-9590 F +1 078-283-2742 www.QuartoKnows.com

A CIP record for this book is available from the Library of Congress.

ISBN 978-0-7112-6287-4

The illustrations were created digitally
Set in Granjon
Published and edited by Georgia Amson-Bradshaw
Designed by Zoë Tucker
Production by Dawn Cameron

Manufactured in the USA by Jostens on recycled FSC® paper, JO022021

9 8 7 6 5 4 3 2 1

31192022194979